# Catie Copley's
# Great Escape

*written by* Deborah Kovacs
*illustrated by* Jared T. Williams

DAVID R. GODINE, PUBLISHER
BOSTON

Pour notre famille canadienne.  D.K.

To my father, who showed me the beauty of a well-told story, the
value of hard work, and the strength of patience. J.T.W.

First published in 2009 by
DAVID R. GODINE · *Publisher*
Post Office Box 450
Jaffrey, New Hampshire 03452
*www.godine.com*

LIBRARY OF CONGRESS CATALOGING-IN-PUBLICATION DATA

Kovacs, Deborah.
Catie Copley's great escape / by Deborah Kovacs ; illustrated by Jared T. Williams.
p.  cm.
Summary: Catie, canine ambassador at a Boston hotel, meets a new friend
and shows him her city, then accompanies him to the Quebec City, Canada, hotel
where he works, enjoying many new experiences before returning home with Jim.
ISBN 978-1-56792-379-7 – ISBN 978-1-56792-382-7
1. Service dogs—Juvenile fiction.  [1. Service dogs—Fiction.  2. Dogs—Fiction.
3. Voyages and travels—Fiction. 4. Hotels, motels, etc.—Fiction.
5. Boston (Mass.)—Description and travel—Fiction.  6. Québec (Québec)—Fiction.
7. Canada—Fiction.]  I. Williams, Jared T., ill.  II. Title.
PZ10.3.K8453Cbg 2009
[E]—dc22
2008046917

FIRST EDITION
*Printed in China*

I was enjoying an afternoon nap in the lobby of the Copley Plaza, the beautiful hotel where I spend my days. My best friend, Jim the concierge, was close by. Everything was just the way I like it — busy and familiar.

But change was in the air.

"Wake up, Catie," said Jim.

"Someone is here to see you."

"Wuuf," said an unfamiliar voice.

I opened one eye.

The wet nose of a furry dog was
a few inches from mine.

"This is Santol," said Jim. "He
works at a big hotel, the Château
Frontenac, in Quebec City.
That's all the way up in Canada.
He trained to be a guide dog, just
like you. He is here for a visit."

Santol snatched my toy lobster,

shaking it at me with a playful growl. Then he scooted away with it

across the lobby. He crouched and grinned at me, wanting to play.

"Let's take Santol for a walk," said Jim.

"Wuuf!" said Santol.

Jim took us across busy Copley Square. It was Farmers' Market day.
I smelled fresh bread, fresh cheese, and Concord grapes.

Pigeons were everywhere.

I wanted to chase them, but I am too well behaved.

What about Santol? I peeked at him.

He was still grinning. But he was being good too.

This time, I grinned back.

Jim took us for a romp on Boston Common.

Santol met some of my friends:

Sam the Bassett Hound;

Rorschach the mutt;

Drew the Great Dane;

and Lindy, the Springer Spaniel.

We played a long game of Chase Me, Chase You.

By the end, we were completely pooped.

And Santol and I were pals.

In the morning, it was time for Santol to go home.

Jim was going to drive him back. I was sad to see him go.

But then, I had a wonderful surprise.

Jim opened the car door and said, "Hop in, Catie! You can come too."

I don't bark often, but I did bark then. Twice.

Santol and I sat in the back of Jim's big car.

Jim opened the windows just enough so we could catch all the new smells.

Then we hit the road!

The drive from Boston to Quebec is long and interesting.

There is something different to see around every curve.

In the morning, we stopped to climb a mountain.

At noon, we had a tasty picnic beside a beautiful covered bridge.

In the afternoon, we swam in a cold, clear pond.

Then we rolled in the crackling leaves to dry off.

Finally, we got to Quebec City, Santol's home.

I think my hotel is big, but Santol's hotel is GIGANTIC.

From the outside, it looks like a mountain with windows.

I met Santol's person, Geneviève. Santol was very happy to see her.

"I have to go now," said Jim. "But I will be back in two days. Geneviève and Santol will take good care of you." Then he was gone. And I was alone with my new friend. Geneviève put my bed right next to Santol's. Santol cuddled up close beside me. Listening to him breathe calmed me down. Soon I was asleep.

When I woke up in the morning, Santol was ready to play.

We visited his favorite places — the sunny room where people eat, looking out over the big, broad St. Lawrence river and the busy kitchen with smells as delicious as my hotel's kitchen in Boston.

My favorite place of all was a couch on the second floor next to a warm fireplace. (I don't think we were supposed to sit on the couch, but no one saw us. Besides, we were very careful and didn't leave even a speck of fur behind.)

We went out to see the town.

I met Santol's friends Jeanne, the cart horse, whose hooves go
clip-clop, clip-clop on the old streets and Jean, her driver.

I met Bâtisse, the regimental goat.

I also met Monique,

the apple-juggler . . .

who dropped some of her apples . . .

which we tried to fetch . . . but they rolled down some stairs . . .

actually, a L O T of stairs . . . exactly one hundred and seventy. (I am very good

at counting.) Once we caught up with the apples, we were in

the lower part of the Old City.

The streets in the Old City are made of stones called "cobbles."
The buildings are very old and pretty.

I smelled something
both different and familiar,
and definitely delicious.
Geneviève called it a
"*saucisson*."
She gave some
to me and
Santol to share.
No matter what
she called it, I know a sausage when I taste one! We rode back up the hill
in a big glass box called a "*funiculaire*."

That evening, we took a walk on the Promenade.

It was very crowded.

Everyone kept saying, *"Feu d'artifice! Feu d'artifice!"*

I did not understand them. I wish I had.

I don't mind being in big crowds, but I really don't like loud noises.

I heard an ENORMOUS sound and saw bright lights in the sky over the river!

I was so surprised and so scared, I yelped and jumped.

My leash came unhooked from my collar. I ran away.

Soon I was lost among all the people.

The sounds kept getting louder.

I had to get out of there!

I ran until I was far away from the loud bangs and crashes.

Soon I was in a lonely part of town that I had never seen before.

I was lost.

I sat down and wondered what to do.

I tried to be brave.

Then, I heard a clip-clop, clip-clop that sounded familiar.

It was Santol's friends, Jean and Jeanne!

"*Pauvre Catie!*" said Jean. "*Viens ici!*" He patted the seat next to him.

I knew just what he meant and jumped right up.

Jean and Jeanne took me all the way back to the hotel.

Santol and Geneviève rushed up to us. They had been very worried.

Santol sniffed me everywhere.

Geneviève kept patting my head and saying,

*"Merci! Merci beaucoup!"* over and over to Jean and Jeanne.

After my long day. I went right to sleep.

I dreamed I was back in Boston, chasing the pigeons on Boston Common.

In the morning, I woke up to find a familiar hand scratching me behind the ears. I opened my eyes. Jim smiled at me. "Time to go home, Catie," he said. I was so happy to see him, I barked THREE times!

It was sad to say goodbye to Santol and Geneviève.

But I am always happy when I am with Jim.

Snow began to fall as we headed to Jim's car.

"Winter's coming Catie," said Jim. I wagged my tail.

Winter is the coziest time of the year.

Now I am back in my busy lobby, near my best friend.

Sometimes I dream about Santol and his beautiful hotel.

But mostly I curl up and smile, because I am exactly where I want to be.